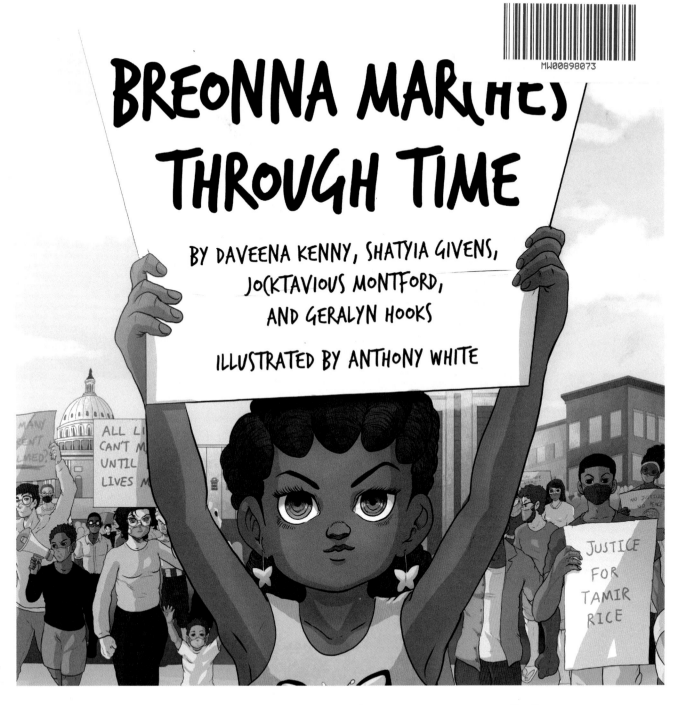

BREONNA MAR(HE) THROUGH TIME

BY DAVEENA KENNY, SHATYIA GIVENS,
JOCKTAVIOUS MONTFORD,
AND GERALYN HOOKS

ILLUSTRATED BY ANTHONY WHITE

Reach Incorporated | Washington, DC
Shout Mouse Press

Reach Education, Inc. / Shout Mouse Press
Published by
Shout Mouse Press, Inc.

Shout Mouse Press is a nonprofit writing and publishing program dedicated to amplifying underheard voices. This book was produced through Shout Mouse workshops and in collaboration with Shout Mouse artists and editors.

Shout Mouse invites young people from marginalized backgrounds to tell their own stories in their own voices and, as published authors, to act as leaders and agents of change. In partnership with other mission-aligned nonprofits, we are building a catalog of inclusive books that ensure that all children can see themselves represented on the page. Our 300+ authors have produced original children's books, comics, novels, memoirs, and poetry collections.

Learn more and see our full catalog at www.shoutmousepress.org.

For all the kids whose voices are never heard.
Now is the time to make a change.

And for Breonna Taylor.

AUTHORS' NOTE

This book was inspired by **Marilyn Luper Hildreth**.
At eight years old, Hildreth suggested protesting segregation,
or the forced separation of Black people from white people,
by sitting at the Katz Drugstore lunch counter in Oklahoma City.
This suggestion led to some of the first sit-ins
of the Civil Rights Movement.

The first time I learned I could time travel was the day I knew my community was in trouble. Let me tell you the story...

I live in Washington, DC. Southeast DC, if you wanna be specific. And I do.

Most summer days, everyone on my street would be outside enjoying themselves. We all knew each other. We always connected. We would go to Sweets and Treats and get oatmeal cream pies. Or we would go to the truck and get hot sausages and seeds.

But this was not most summers.

This summer, stores are boarded up, and the ice cream truck doesn't come around anymore.

Instead of hearing the truck's song, we hear police sirens. Voices on megaphones chant, "Black Lives Matter!" The people who I love don't come around anymore either. Now it's just my mom, my dad, and my older brother Brandon.

This summer, we're all stuck at home, and people are feeling down. My mom used to go outside and water her garden. My dad used to laugh and joke with the neighbors. Brandon used to go to the court with his friends to play basketball.

Now, all my family does is watch the news and say, "Oh Lord."

And all I do is stay in the house and miss my friends. There's so much going on, and we're all feeling helpless. How is anything going to change?

I just want to get my community back.

PEACEFUL PROTESTS EMERGE FOLLOWING GEORGE FLOYD INCIDENT

One day, I am watching TV with my family. I see lots of different kinds of people — different colors, different ages, some even as young as I am. They are holding posters with faces on them, faces that look like the people I know. I hear *NO JUSTICE, NO PEACE!*

And all of a sudden, things go black...

When I wake up, I am on a city street. I see old-fashioned cars that make a lot of noise. Everyone I see is wearing suits or long dresses. I don't recognize anything. "Where am I?"

I look around and see signs that say "whites only." They're everywhere. The public restrooms. The movie theater. Water fountains. A drugstore with the name "Katz."

Everything starts spinning. I need to find safety. I see a nearby church with no sign. I go inside.

Inside, I see a young Black girl speaking at the front of the church. She looks as old as I am. She's speaking to a group of kids who are captivated by what she is saying. They say, "Wooo," and "Take your time, Marilyn!"

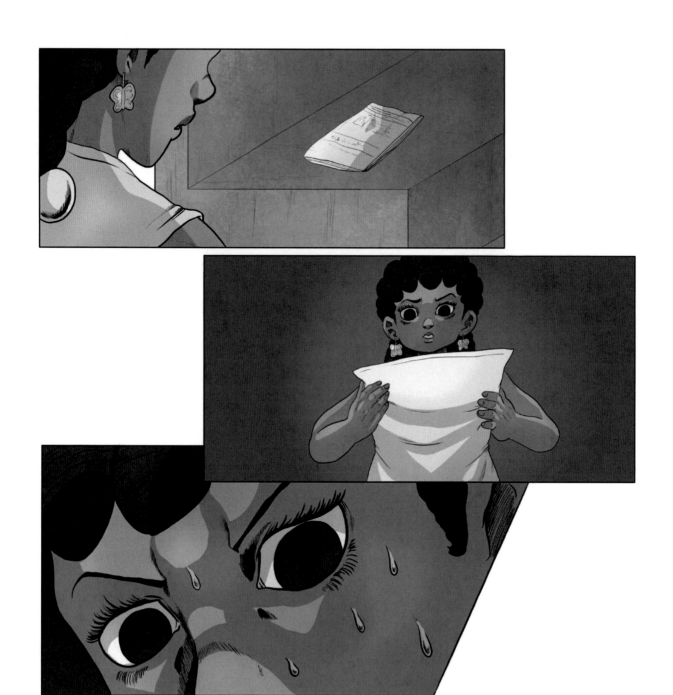

I look down and see a newspaper on the pew called *The Daily Oklahoman*. The date on it is November 17, 1955.

How did I get here? And more importantly, how am I going to get back?

I need to sit down.

"NAACP Youth Council, I am tired of segregation!" says the girl. "All people should be equal. We're supposed to be unified, not divided."

"Mmmmhmmm," says a lady in the pew in front of me.

"So I have an idea," continues the girl. "How about we go down to Katz Drug Store and just sit? Just sit at their 'whites only' lunch counter until they serve us?"

People begin to whisper. I watch and think, *This idea would actually take someone's breath away! How can someone so small hold so much power?*

"We demand equal rights NOW!" says the girl. "Our goal is a peaceful movement to break down the fence of discrimination and segregation!"

Watching her, I am determined to have a great impact on others as well. And as I think about how I can make a change, I hear chanting.

NO JUSTICE, NO PEACE! NO JUSTICE, NO PEACE!

And again, everything goes black...

When I wake up, things look familiar, but also changed. Sweets and Treats is now luxury apartments. Where the ice cream truck would park, there is now a vegan restaurant.

What is happening? What happened to my community?

The wind blows a magazine my way. It reads "July 2025."

I start to hear voices, and I follow them down the street. "Say his name! Brandon! Remember his voice! Black Lives Matter."

This is still going on? I think. I walk closer and see a familiar face on the signs. It's my brother!

I start to worry — *Is Brandon in danger?! Is he OK?! How can I make sure he stays safe?* I can't let this keep happening to my community.

I hear, *NO JUSTICE, NO PEACE! NO JUSTICE...* And everything goes black...

JUST[ ]ICE FOR BRANDON

When I wake up, I am home again. My family is wearing the same clothes from before. I look around, wondering if they notice anything out of the ordinary. They don't. They are focused on the TV and the protests.

I step in front of the TV to block their view. "I went back in time!" I say excitedly. "I met a young activist named Marilyn. She was the same age as me and had the same skin color as me. She was powerful, young, and brave. She inspired me to stand up for my community. So, from now on, this is what I will do!"

My parents look at each other. They look concerned. My brother looks surprised. "You got an active imagination, sis," he says.

"Imagination or not," my father says, "you are our daughter, Breonna, and we want to support you. We want to make a change, too."

So, the next day, we finally GO to a protest instead of watching them on TV. My mother's voice rises up in flames as she chants. My father passes out water bottles to the other protesters. My brother protects me as I march.

And I do! I march proudly and alongside my family, alongside my community like I marched throughout time. I feel like I am a part of history, like I am building a better future, like I am helping the world.

I walk to the front of the group and see a stage. I wave at the speaker behind the microphone. He sees my passion and gestures for me to come over. I look around and smile, stepping up to the podium.

I hear Marilyn's voice in my head: *All people should be equal. We're supposed to be unified, not divided...*

As the crowd settles, I make one hand into a fist. "I am ready to make a change and get our community back... Are you?"

ABOUT THE AUTHORS

DAVEENA KENNY

My name Is Daveena Kenny. I am 15 years old and a sophomore at Coolidge Senior High School. I like to dance and cheer. I wrote this book because I want children to be able to talk about what's going on in their daily lives, and to discuss why Black people are in the position we are in. I hope readers understand that you can change things in this world. You can always help out the people you love.

SHATYIA GIVENS

My name is Shatyia Givens, and I am a sophomore at H.D. Woodson High School. I am 15 years old. My favorite activities are drawing, reading, and cooking. This is my first book. I hope that my young readers recognize that someone like you can have a huge impact on others, whether big or small. I hope this story inspires you to be a better person, and to always stand up for what you believe in.

JOCKTAVIOUS MONTFORD

My name is Jock Montford, and I am a junior at Ballou Senior High School. I play on the basketball team and my favorite subject is math. This is my second book with Reach and Shout Mouse; I also co-wrote *Georgia in the Jungle* (2019). By writing this book I hope that kids of all ages can learn about our past, present, and future. I hope they can have a different perspective and take a stand for Black lives.

GERALYN HOOKS

My name is Geralyn Hooks, GiGi for short. I'm a 16-year-old junior at Anacostia High School. Outside of school, I enjoy hanging out with friends and shopping. I hope to build on my love of people through a career in psychology or sociology. I want young readers of our book to know that just because they're little doesn't mean they can't make a difference in the world.

ALEXA PATRICK served as Story Coach for this book.

HAYES DAVIS served as Head Story Coach for this year's series.

ABOUT THE ILLUSTRATOR

ANTHONY WHITE

Anthony White is a comic book artist and animator studying in the Kinetic Imaging program at VCUarts. He hopes to work in the illustration industry and/or on a serialized television program. He hopes that his art can help the fight for change move forward just as much as words can. His art within this book was inspired by the heroic efforts of the peaceful protests all around the world and by Chadwick Boseman.

WRITERS AND ARTISTS
AT WORK

ACKNOWLEDGMENTS

For the eighth summer in a row, teens from Reach Incorporated were issued a challenge: compose original children's books that will both educate and entertain young readers. Specifically, these teens were asked to create inclusive stories that reflect their lived experiences — experiences that this year include the current global pandemic and the struggle for racial justice. As always, these teens have demonstrated that they know their audience, they believe in their mission, and they take pride in the impact they can make on young lives.

Thirteen writers spent the month of July brainstorming ideas, generating potential plots, writing, revising, and providing critiques. Authoring quality books is challenging work at any time, but this year, these young people had to collaborate virtually, during a COVID-19 shutdown. These authors have our immense gratitude and respect: Jocktavious, Daveena, Geralyn, Shatyia, Japan, Damarco, Emilie, Riley, Anthony, Diarou, Danya, Joseph, and Samaria.

These books represent a collaboration between Reach Incorporated and Shout Mouse Press, and we are grateful for the leadership provided by members of both teams. From Reach, Anyssa Dhaouadi, Victoria Feathersone, and Charles Walker contributed meaningfully to discussions and morale, and the Reach summer program leadership of Jusna Perrin kept us organized and connected, even while we all worked apart. From the Shout Mouse Press team, we thank Head Story Coach Hayes Davis, who oversaw this year's workshops, and Story Coaches Barrett Smith, Sarai Johnson, Faith Campbell, and Alexa Patrick for bringing both fun and insight to the project. We can't thank enough illustrators Camryn Simms, Anthony White, Alex Perkins, and Rob Gibsun for bringing these stories to life with their beautiful artwork. Finally, Amber Colleran brought a keen eye and important mentorship to the project as the series Art Director and book designer. We are grateful for the time and talents of these writers and artists!

Finally, we thank those of you who have purchased books and cheered on our authors. It is your support that makes it possible for these teen authors to engage and inspire young readers. We hope you smile as much while you read as these teens did while they wrote.

Mark Hecker,
Reach Incorporated

Kathy Crutcher,
Shout Mouse Press

ABOUT REACH INCORPORATED

Reach Incorporated develops readers and leaders by preparing teens to serve as tutors and role models for younger students, resulting in improved literacy outcomes for both the teen tutors and their elementary school students.

Founded in 2009, Reach recruits high school students to be elementary school reading tutors. After completing a year in our program, teens gain access to additional leadership development opportunities, including The Summer Leadership Academy and The College Mentorship Program. All of this exists within our unique, college and career preparation framework, The Reach Fellowship. Through this comprehensive system of supports, teens are prepared to thrive in high school and beyond.

Through their work as reading tutors, our teens noticed that the books they read with their students did not always reflect their lived experiences. As always, we felt the best way we could address this issue was to put our teens in charge. Through our collaboration with Shout Mouse Press, these teens create engaging stories with diverse characters that invite young readers to explore the world through words. By purchasing our books, you support student-led, community-driven efforts to improve educational outcomes in the District of Columbia.

LEARN MORE AT WWW.REACHINCORPORATED.ORG.

Made in the USA
Monee, IL
07 November 2020